JOURNEY TO **STAR WARS**: THE RISE OF SKYWALKER

## STAR WARS™

### FIRST ORDER VILLAINS

WRITTEN BY MICHAEL SIGLAIN

ILLUSTRATED BY DIOGO SAITO & LUIGI AIMÉ

DISNEY

LUCASFILM

PRESS

LOS ANGELES · NEW YORK

Printed in the United States of America

First Edition, October 2019   10 9 8 7 6 5 4 3 2

Library of Congress Control Number on file

FAC-029261-19284

ISBN 978-1-368-05244-3

Visit the official *Star Wars* website at: www.starwars.com.

SUSTAINAB
FORESTRY
INITIATIVE
Certified Sourcing
www.sfiprogram.org
SFI-01415

The galaxy is at war.

The First Order,
led by the evil Kylo Ren,
wants to rule over all.

But the Resistance,
led by General Leia Organa,
wants freedom for the galaxy.

Kylo Ren is powerful in the
dark side of the Force.
The Force is a mystical energy field
that binds the galaxy together.
It can be used for good or evil.

Kylo Ren uses the Force for evil.
Kylo is skilled with a lightsaber,
a laser sword that he made himself.

Kylo learned about the dark side from a shadowy figure named Snoke. Snoke was once the Supreme Leader of the First Order.

Under Supreme Leader Snoke,
the First Order built a deadly
weapon called the Starkiller.
The Starkiller had enough power
to destroy entire planets.

The Resistance attacked the
Starkiller . . .

. . . and destroyed the weapon.
But that did not stop
the First Order.
And it did not stop Kylo Ren.

Kylo Ren wanted more power,
so he defeated Snoke.
Now Kylo leads the First Order.
The First Order wants to control
the galaxy.

Kylo also leads the deadly
and mysterious Knights of Ren.

Little is known about
the Knights of Ren.
But they are loyal only to Kylo.

General Hux commands
the First Order's army of
stormtroopers.

Stormtroopers are
dangerous soldiers.
They are tough, mean, and loyal.

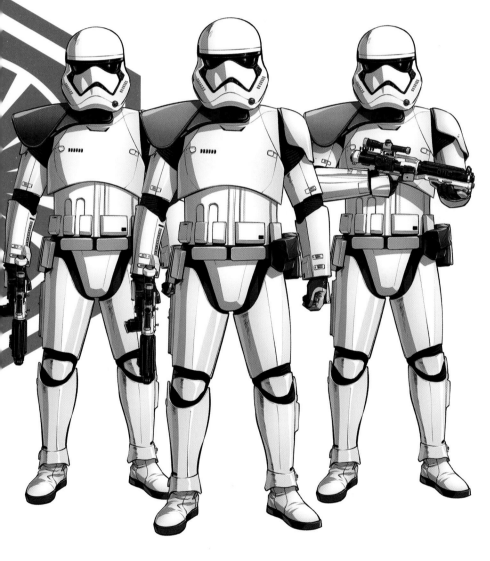

Some stormtroopers wear
special armor.

Other troopers carry
special weapons.

Red Sith troopers
guard Kylo Ren.
The Sith are strong in the
dark side of the Force.

Sith jet troopers fly
with rocket packs.

The First Order travels through space
in giant ships called Star Destroyers.
Some Star Destroyers are larger
and more powerful than others.

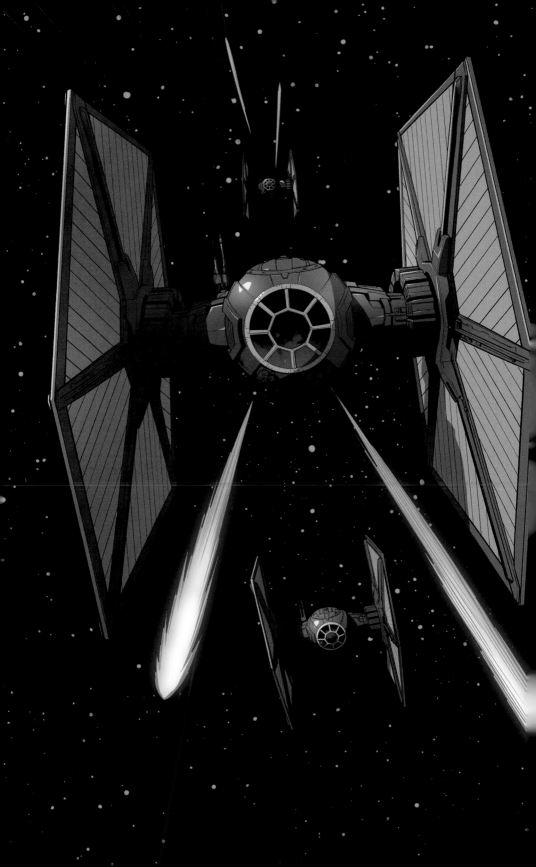

Twin ion engine fighters,
called TIE fighters,
are fast starfighters
flown by First Order pilots.

On the ground, the First Order uses
big machines that walk on four legs.
These machines carry soldiers
and can stomp over anything.

They are called AT-ATs or walkers.
The First Order also uses larger and
more dangerous machines
called gorilla walkers.

But Kylo Ren will need more than
troopers and ships to
defeat the Resistance.
Kylo will need to defeat Rey.
Rey is one of the Resistance's
most powerful heroes.

Rey is strong in the light side
of the Force.
Kylo has battled Rey before,
and he is ready to face her again.

Kylo will let nothing—
and no one—
stand in the way of
the First Order!